Can you find the mouse in every scene?

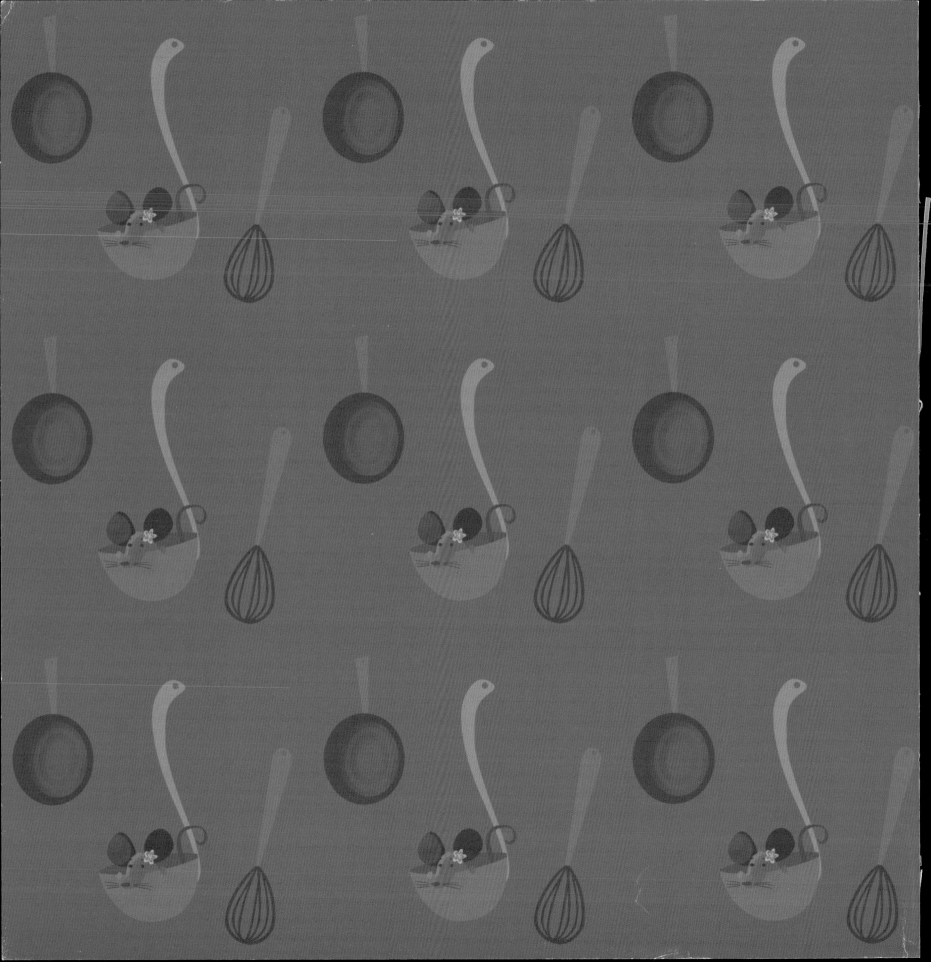

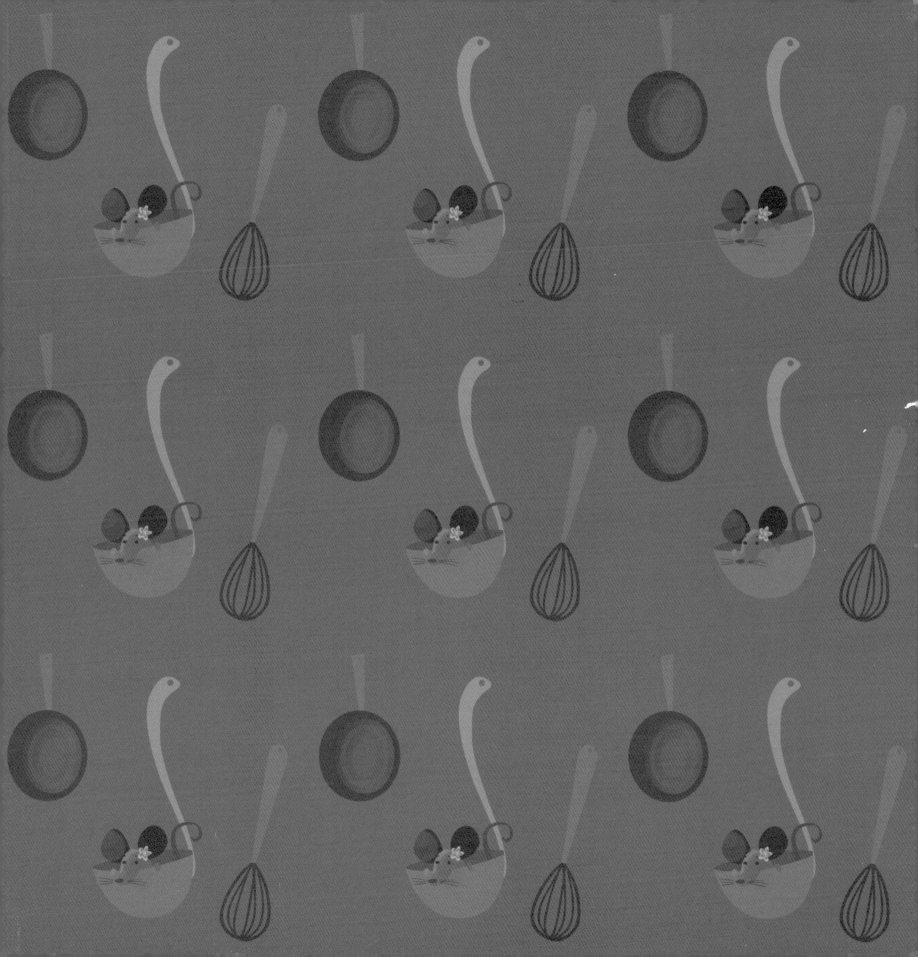

Published by Top That! Publishing plc
Tide Mill Way, Woodbridge, Suffolk, IP12 1AP, UK
www.topthatpublishing.com
Text copyright © 2013 Enid Richemont
Illustrations copyright © 2013 Top That! Publishing plc
All rights reserved
0 2 4 6 8 9 7 5 3 1
Printed and bound in China

Creative Director – Simon Couchman
Editorial Director – Daniel Graham

Written by Enid Richemont
Illustrated by Tiago Americo

ISBN 978-1-78244-189-2

A catalogue record for this book is available from the British Library
Printed and bound in China

...and Nobody Noticed the Mouse

by Enid Richemont

'For Jude and Alan, with love.'
Enid Richemont

There was going to be a
very grand wedding ...

... but nobody noticed the mouse.

Hymn
Book
✝

Flowers were brought into the very grand church – lilies and roses and tulips and ivy ...

... but nobody noticed the mouse.

The mouse scuttled
up to the organ loft ...

... but nobody noticed the mouse.

The mouse stood on one of the organ pipes ...

... but nobody noticed the mouse.

The bride and
her bridesmaids
came into the church ...

... and still nobody noticed the mouse.

The organist played
and the mouse was
blown ...

WHOOOSH ...

... onto a posh lady's hat.

THUD

Then they all went off
to a grand hotel ...

... and nobody noticed the mouse.

The mouse ate his fill, then went off to sleep,
and nobody noticed the mouse ...

- TOMATO
- BANANAS

- SPAGHETTI
CARBONARA

- LASAGNA
- TABLE ③

... except the lady
mouse who lived in the kitchen.
She **CERTAINLY** noticed the mouse!

They were married behind a big barrel of flour,
where nobody noticed the mice.

And they lived happily
and had lots of
babies, until ...

... one day a
waitress squealed,

'MICE!'

So the mice and their
babies went to live
in the garden ...

... where nobody
noticed the mice!

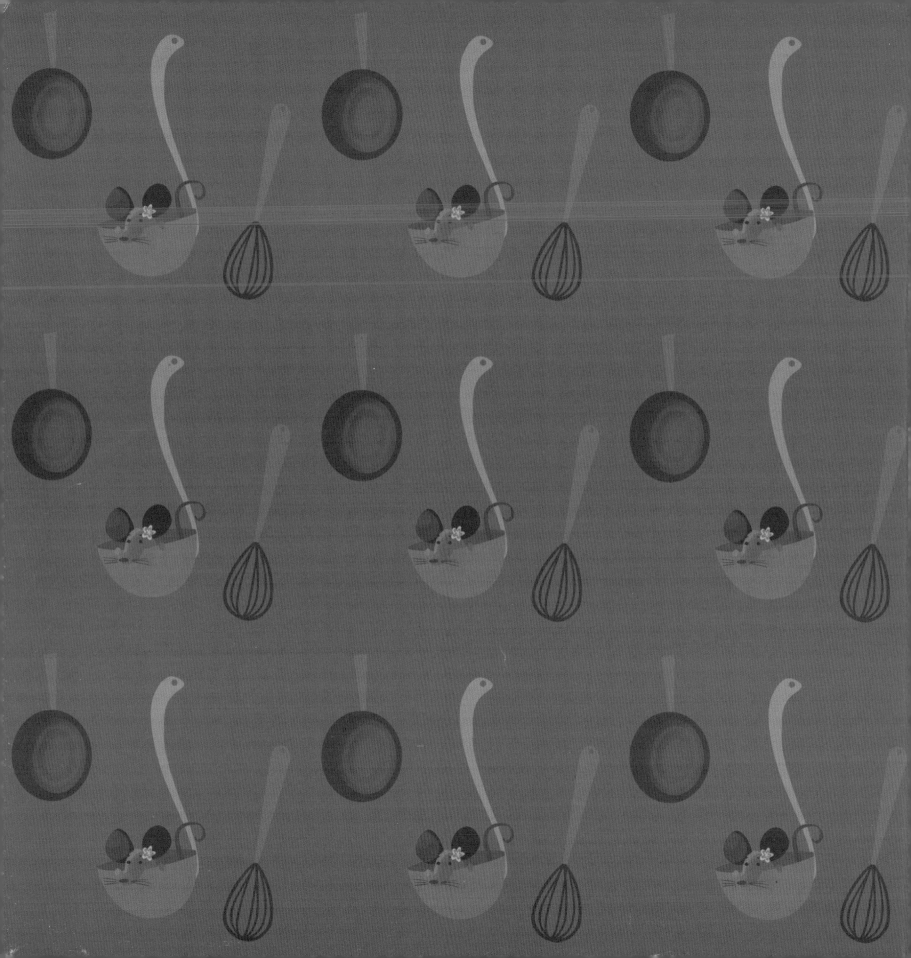

More great picture books from Top That! Publishing

ISBN 978-1-78244-064-2

A rhyming storybook, full of nonsense, by inimitable author, Edward Lear.

ISBN 978-1-78244-073-4

This tale, full of fun and folly, recalls the Quangle Wangle and his delightful hat.

ISBN 978-1-84956-778-7

A fantastical tale about a boy and the adventures he has with his rocking horse.

ISBN 978-1-78244-040-6

Follow the little raindrop's adventure and learn all about the water cycle.

ISBN 978-1-78244-059-8

Peter's pebbles come to life in this perfectly crafted tale, full of imagination.

ISBN 978-1-78244-074-1

Cammy the colourful chameleon learns an important lesson in this vibrant tale.

ISBN 978-1-78244-170-0

Something mysterious is following poor kitty. Whatever can it be?

ISBN 978-1-78244-158-8

A humorous story written in the classic pirate song tradition.

ISBN 978-1-78244-109-0

Search the beautifully illustrated tale to find the hidden ghosts.

ISBN 978-1-78244-187-8

A heartwarming tale about the magic of children's love and creativity.

ISBN 978-1-84956-438-0

A fantastical tale about unruly morning hair and a mischievous fairy.

ISBN 978-1-84956-439-7

The animal food chain is turned upside-down in this funny story with a twist.

Available from all good bookstores or visit www.topthatpublishing.com
Look for Top That! Apps in the Apple iTunes Store